ISBN-13: 978-1511616171
ISBN-10: 1511616172

Printed in the U.S.A.
The edition first printing, October 2011
The edition second Printing, November 2018

Gypsy Meadow

WRITTEN AND ILLUSTRATED BY: J.T. GRIFFIN

CO-WRITTEN: MADISON BROWN

To my Daughter -

Years have passed and I will never forget the love that we shared with Gypsy and Bambi. Writing this book with you when you were young, is memories that will never fade in my heart. This is when you met your forever girl, Abby. Sometimes things happen and animals move on just to make room for the animals that need it more. I am so incredibly proud of you, and that your love for horses will never die. They leave hoof prints on our hearts, just like you leave a trail of life in my heart.

Love you dearly, Mom

A young girl stood at the corner of the fence watching a wild horse leap through the air. Her parents thought the mare was a wild beast, and not fit for a child. The little girl saw the beautiful gray

Arabian in a different way. She understood the horse's defensive manner. She recognized the horse's strong will, protecting her damaged soul. The little girl knew that the mare only wished to be loved by someone. The young girl saw the scars on the mare's legs, which only made her want her more.

She could only see a horse that was meant to be her very own. She chose the lost, "Gypsy."

I stand here at the corner of the fence enjoying the taste of a fresh apple, as my little girl watches me chew. I didn't always have a chance to enjoy such a grand thing.
We don't get to choose our people like people to get to choose us. This is the first person that I have grown to trust. She understands me and accepts my spirit, and understands why I am shy at quick movements. She thinks I am beautiful inside and out.
I choose to let my little girl love me.

I stand here at the corner of the fence as I watch my little girl jump off the bus. She runs to me, dropping her bag and wraps her arms around my neck. I see my horse friends. I follow my feel knowing that we are going to ride and see new places. I stand patiently as my girls put the saddle on my back. She climbs on my back and turns me toward an unfamiliar trail. I feel safe with her guiding me, even though the sounds and smell are unusual. We fly with the wind along the ocean's shore. I can hear the other horses hoof beats as they excitedly prance behind me.

I remember when I would have feared what was behind me; now I trust my little girl will keep us safe.

I choose the young girl that rides gracefully on my back.

I stand here at the corner of the fence watching a large trailer come towards me. I then see my young girl dressed in her best western carrying my brand new show saddle. I meet her at the gate knowing that we will have a day of
fun in the ring.

I remember when, I would have run and hidden, fearful that the trailer would take me yet to another home. I know now that this is my home.

I choose the young girl that makes me feel secure.

I stand here at the corner of the fence watching a load of hay comes towards the barn. I gallop around the pasture in glee. I remember when I felt desperate and fought for just one bite. At one time I had forgotten the taste of "fresh cut" hay. I choose the young lady that keeps me healthy and happy through the years.

I stand here at the corner of the fence watching a young man walk towards me with my grown girl.

I remember when I would have walked away in fear, but now I have learned how to trust again I know now that I must share my young lady with this young man. I trust that he will never harm her. I let him touch and rub my face.

I choose the young woman that looks for my opinion in a major decision.

I stand here at the corner of the fence, as I watch my person pack up my things into the trailer. She comes and kisses me and tells me that I am coming to our new home.
I remember when I would have fought for freedom, fearing that I would be taken to another terrible home.
I choose the woman that takes me with her.

I   stand here at the corner of my new fence smelling my person's large belly knowing that there will be a little person to love and trust.
I remember when I would have been worried to love another as much as I love my person.
I choose the woman that teaches me to lose more than one.

I stand her at the corner of the fence watching my lady bring out riding gear. We ride through the meadow. I feel my aging bones are growing weaker. We both know that this will be our the last ride together.
I remember when I chose not to be ridden because I could not trust the person on my back. I feared that they would hurt and scare me.
I choose to accept a comfortable life in the meadows, with no worries or expectations.

I stand here at the corner of the fence as my person introduces me to a beautiful little girl. I smell her knowing that her life is brand new and there are so many new responsibilities to share.

I remember when I would have run from a strange person fearing that I may be hurt.

I choose to love two people.

I stand here at the corner of the fence as I watch a young girl jump off the bus. She runs to me dropping her bag and wraps her arms around my neck. She pulls a fresh apple from her bag. I take the apple with no hesitation enjoying each and every bite. I hold my head low in her arms as, as she reminds me of another young girl that found me years ago.

I remember when I wasn't so lucky to have someone to love me. I now understand the true meaning of love.
I choose my life enjoying the tender hugs and kisses that I so happy to receive every day.

I stand here at the corner of the fence as I watch the young girl pull a saddle towards me. My person and the young girl gently places the saddle on my back. My lady smiles and hugs me around my neck, as though to say, "Now it is my little girls turn." The little girl climbs on my back as I took my new love for her very first ride. I gently pace along the fence listening to her laughter and excitement, as she gracefully held onto my mane.

I remember when I took my little girl for her first ride. I remember the fear and the unsettled feeling, afraid she would hurt me; but then her loving touch made it easier for me to trust her. I feel the same trust with this little girl.

I choose to spend the rest of my days with two people that helped me find spirit within.

I stand here at the corner of the fence watching a trailer arrive at my barn. I watch a shiny chestnut mare and a small shaggy pony prance into my pasture. I remember when I would have made my territory well known and not accept any new friends. This day I choose my new barn family.

I stand here at the corner of the fence,
I watch my people enjoy a long ride
through the meadow, with the
chestnut mare, "Flash" and the
fuzzy pony, "Bambi", following
closely behind. I see the little girl
smile in excitement. My person
gracefully rides Flash, with a
familiar look of happiness on
her face.
I remember the long rides that
I shared with my person. I hope
Bambi and Flash realize how lucky
they are to be loved. I know my old
bones couldn't take the long strolls in the
meadow, my time was short and my expectations
were retired.
I choose my family and the safe surroundings that I have
found. I know that my family has given me the best gift that
any creature could have – A home.

I stand here at the corner of my fence as my person places wraps around my legs and medicine in my eyes. I knew that my person was trying to help my swelling and loss of sight.
I remember when nobody cared that I was in pain.
I chose my family who cares enough about me to make sure I am loved and well. Even though my sight is gone, their images will never fade from my mind.

I stand here at the corner of my fence watching from above, my person laying with me in the meadow, telling me that it is okay to let go. Her tears flow on my cheek, as I know she will keep me safe in her heart. I watch myself lay in the meadow, as her sobs make it hard for me to understand.

I see my young girl watching her mother's heartbreak, in the distance. One day, I will see her in her dreams, I will still watch through my heart.

I remember the first day we met; she looked beyond my flaws and chose me. I choose the person that saved me and taught me how to love and trust again.

I stand here at the corner of my fence, as I watch my two loves ride through the meadow, only to see that my friend Bambi is having trouble keeping up as she used too.

I remember when Bambi's illness was held off by the love of her girl.
I choose for my friend to heal and feel the love for a longer period of time.

I stand here at the corner of the fence, looking over my friend Bambi and her little girl laying in the meadow. Bambi finds herself resting more often these days. The little girl kisses her over and over again, knowing that her time is limited.
I remember laying in a meadow with my young girl, understanding the feeling of true love.
I choose for Bambi, to enjoy the small things in life.

I stand here at the corner of the fence, watching my friend Bambi enjoy her best moments with her young girl. Bambi feels lucky to find such a loving young girl. Bambi knows that this is the time that she needs love the most. Bambi's bad health has caught up with her. She tries to follow her young girl, but her painful hooves would not allow her too.

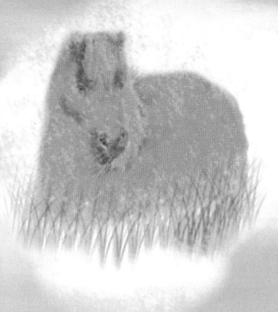

I remember when Bambi and I ate together in the meadows. I remember when she found love and trust in her young girl. I remember when Bambi waited at the edge of the fence for her little girl to run from the bus, wrapping her arms around her neck. I remember Bambi following her young girl through the meadow, knowing that the little girl would show her new adventures. I know that Bambi has found love and that is all that she needed.

I choose to help her find me again, as I wait for her at the end of the meadow.

They stand at the corner of the fence looking over the meadow, as the tears slowly stream down their cheeks. The mother grabs her daughter's hand and whispers to her.

"I remember when they ran through the meadows, I remember when we found love and I remember how

Gypsy and Bambi changed our lives."
We choose for them to run together again.
We choose to feel their hoof prints in our hearts because we feel as though they loved us as we loved them. They are together again, and we shall feel proud that we had the chance to share our love; with them and we know that we gave them the life that they deserved.

Gypsy and Bambi stand at the corner of the fence looking over the meadow. They watch us, the young girl jumps off the bus, wrapping her arms around Flash's neck. She pulls a fresh apple from her bag, as she watches her chew.

They remember when Flash would have never considered a child as her best friend. They know that Flash found her love, not only from one person but from two.

They chose to pass on their love to the young girl, and her new horse.

They stand watching over the meadow, watching over what they know will never fade from their minds, for an image that will never perish in their hearts.

Dear Readers,

Losing a pet is a heartbreaking moment, we feel as though we lost a member of our family. Because really, we have. But, the truth is, we made that animal a part of a family, they move on to make room for another pet to be part of your family. They are leaving stepping stones along the way and giving others a chance to be loved. Flash passed on May 13, 2016, she lived to her peak age of 36, almost reaching Gypsy's age of 37. It is not about the few years that we have with them, it is the memories we create, and the time we give and second chances. It is not about making a difference in all pets lives, but one at a time. It counts.

After my daughter and I published this book originally years ago. Through the orginal book she found her love, her name is Abby. Abby was a retired Trotter, that was left in the dust. She was a survivor, and I truly believe that she was survived because she had

a push of hope, knowing she would find her love. She did, we have been enjoying her life, the past seven years. She has pieces of Gypsy in her, and she came to us through this book.

Her too will be a part of Gypsy's Meadow, and we are proud to say she is a part of our family. Owning pets are not ownership, it is opening your heart and your home, to have them part of your family and understanding their past to reach them to the life they deserve. So instead of finding the perfect pet, let the perfect pet find you. Give them the years they have the best they will remember, and if they have gone through many homes, understand they were building their strength to come to find you.

Thank you for support of Gypsy's Meadow

Love from an animal that you gave that second chance to is a love you will never forget.......

Made in the USA
Middletown, DE
30 November 2021

53475627R00020